KU-350-175

DICKENS LIBRARY

The Old
Curiosity Shop

by Charles Dickens

abridged edition

At the Shop

The place was one of those receptacles for old and curious things which seem to crouch in odd corners of this town and to hide their musty treasures from the public eye in jealousy and distrust. There were suits of mail standing like ghosts in armour here and there, fantastic carvings brought from monkish cloisters, rusty weapons of various kinds, distorted figures in china and wood and iron and ivory: tapestry and strange furniture that might have been designed in dreams. The haggard aspect of the little old man was wonderfully suited to the place; he might have groped among old churches and tombs and deserted houses and gathered all the spoils with his own hands. There was nothing in the whole collection but was in keeping with himself; nothing that looked older or more worn than he.

The door opened, a child entered and addressed him as grandfather.

"Why, bless thee, child," said the old man, patting her on the head, "you've been a long time. What if thou missed thy way? What if I had lost thee, Nell."

"I would have found my way back to you, grandfather," said the child boldly; "never fear".

There was a knock at the door and Nell, bursting into a hearty laugh, said it was no doubt dear old Kit come back at last.

Kit was a shock-headed shambling awkward lad with an uncommonly wide mouth, very red cheeks, a turned-up nose, and the most comical expression of face. He was the comedy of the child's life.

"A long way, wasn't it, Kit?" said the little old man.

"Why then, it was a goodish stretch, master," returned Kit.

"Did you find the house easily?"

"Why then, not over and above easy, master," said Kit.

"Of course you have come back hungry?"

"Why then, I do consider myself rather so, master," was the answer.

He carried a large slice of bread and meat and a mug of beer into a corner, and applied himself to disposing of them with great voracity

"Ah!" said the old man, with a sigh. "Come hither, Nell."

The little girl hastened from her seat, and put her arm about his neck.

"Do I love thee, Nell?" said he. "Say – do I love thee, Nell, or no?"

"Indeed, indeed you do," replied the child with great earnestness, "Kit knows you do."

"She is poor now," said the old man, patting the child's cheek, "but I say again that the time is coming when she shall be rich. It has been a long time coming, but it must come at last; a very long time, but it surely must come. It has come to other men who do nothing but waste and riot. When *will* it come to me!"

"I am very happy as I am, grandfather," said the child.

"Tush, tush!" returned the old man, "thou dost not know – how shouldst thou!" Then he muttered between his teeth. And still holding the child between his knees he appeared to be insensible to everything around him.

The child soon occupied herself in preparations for giving Kit a writing lesson, of which it seemed he had a couple every week, and one regularly on that evening, to the great mirth and enjoyment both of himself and his instructress.

The lesson was given – evening passed and night came on – the old man grew restless and impatient – he quitted the house secretly – and the child was left alone within its gloomy walls.

Enter Mr Quilp

Mr Quilp could scarcely be said to be of any particular trade or calling, though his pursuits were diversified and his occupations numerous. He collected the rents of whole colonies of filthy streets and alleys by the waterside, advanced money to the seamen and petty officers of merchant vessels, had a share in the ventures of divers mates of East Indiamen, and smoked his smuggled cigars under the very nose of the Custom House. On the Surrey side of the river was a small rat-infested dreary yard called 'Quilp's Wharf', in which were a little wooden counting-house burrowing all awry in the dust as if it had fallen from the clouds and ploughed into the ground; a few fragments of rusty anchors; several large iron rings; some piles of rotten wood; and two or three heaps of old sheet copper, crumpled, cracked, and battered. On Quilp's Wharf, Daniel Quilp was a ship-breaker, yet to judge from these appearances he must either have been a ship-breaker on a very small scale, or have broken his ships up very small indeed.

It was flood tide when Daniel Quilp sat himself down in the boat to cross to the opposite shore.

Arrived at his destination, the first object that presented itself to his view was a pair of very imperfectly shod feet elevated in the air with the soles upwards, which remarkable appearance was referable to a boy, who being of an eccentric spirit and having a natural taste for tumbling was now standing on his head and contemplating the aspect of the river under these uncommon circumstances. He was speedily brought on his heels by the sound of his master's voice, and as soon as his head was in its right position, Mr Quilp, to speak expressively in the absence of a better verb, 'punched it' for him.

"Come, you let me alone," said the boy, parrying Quilp's hand with both his elbows alternately. "You'll get something you won't like if you don't, and so I tell you."

"You dog," snarled Quilp, "I'll beat you with an iron rod, I'll scratch you with a rusty nail, I'll pinch your eyes, if you talk to me – I will. Now, open the counting-house."

The boy sulkily complied, muttering at first, but desisting when he looked round and saw that Quilp was following him with a steady look.

It was a dirty little box, this counting-house, with nothing in it but an old ricketty desk and two stools, a hat-peg, an ancient almanac, an inkstand with no ink and the stump of one pen, and an eight-day clock which hadn't gone for eighteen years at least and of which the minute-hand had been twisted off for a tooth-pick. Daniel Quilp pulled his hat over his brows, climbed on to the desk (which had a flat top), and stretching his short length upon it (for Quilp was a dwarf) went to sleep with the ease of an old practitioner.

He had not been asleep a quarter of an hour when the boy opened the door and thrust in his head. Quilp was a light sleeper and started up directly.

"Here's somebody for you," said the boy.

"Who?"

"I don't know."

"Ask!" said Quilp, seizing a piece of wood and throwing it at him with such dexterity that it was well the boy disappeared before it reached the spot on which he had stood. "Ask, you dog."

Not caring to venture within range of such missiles again, the boy discreetly sent in his stead the first cause of the interruption, who now presented herself at the door.

"What, Nelly!" cried Quilp.

"Yes," said the child, hesitating whether to enter or retreat, for the dwarf just roused, with his dishevelled hair hanging all about him and a yellow handkerchief over his head, was something fearful to behold; "it's only me, sir."

"Well. Now, come in and shut the door. What's your message, Nelly?"

The child handed him a letter; Mr Quilp, without changing his position further than to turn over a little more on his side and rest his chin on his hand, proceeded to make himself acquainted with its contents.

"Hallo here!" he said at length, in a voice, and with a suddenness, which made the child start as though a gun had been fired off at her ear. "Nelly!"

"Yes, sir."

"Do you know what's inside this letter, Nell?"

"No, sir!"

"Are you sure, quite sure, quite certain, upon your soul?"

"Quite sure, sir."

"Do you wish you may die if you do know, hey?" said the dwarf.

"Indeed I don't know," returned the child.

"Well!" muttered Quilp, as he marked her earnest look. "I believe you. Humph! Gone already? Gone in four-and-twenty hours! What the devil has he done with it, that's the mystery!"

This reflection set him scratching his head and biting his nails once more. While he was thus employed his features gradually relaxed into what was with him a cheerful smile, but which in any other man would have been a ghastly grin of pain.

"Are you tired, Nelly?"

"No, sir. I'm in a hurry to get back, for he will be anxious while I am away."

"There's no hurry, little Nell, no hurry at all," said Quilp.

"I must go back," said the child. "He told me to return directly I had the answer."

The child, overpowered by the weight of her sorrows and anxieties burst into a passion of tears.

"Well," he said, "here's the note. It's only to say that I shall see him tomorrow or maybe next day, and that I couldn't do that little business for him this morning. Goodbye, Nelly."

Nelly, shedding tears, departed.

Nell's Troubles

It was not the monotonous day unchequered by variety and uncheered by pleasant companionship, it was not the dark dreary evenings or the long solitary nights, it was not the absence of every slight and easy pleasure for which young hearts beat high, or the knowing nothing of childhood but its weakness and its easily wounded spirit, that had wrung such tears from Nell. To see her grandfather struck down beneath the pressure of some hidden grief, to mark his wavering and unsettled state, to be agitated at times with a dreadful fear that his mind was wandering, and to trace in his words and looks the dawning of despondent madness; to watch and wait and listen for confirmation of these things day after day, and to feel and know that, come what might, they were alone in the world with no one to help or advise or care about them – these were causes of depression and anxiety that might have sat heavily on an older breast with many influences at work to cheer and gladden it, but how heavily on the mind of a young child to whom they were ever present.

And yet, to the old man's vision, Nell was still the same; there was the same smile for him, the same earnest words, the same merry laugh, the same love and care that sinking deep into his soul seemed to have been present to him through his whole life.

One night, the third after Nelly's interview with Mr Quilp, the old man, who had been weak and ill all day, said he would not leave home that night. The child's eyes sparkled at the intelligence, but her joy subsided when they reverted

13

to his worn and sickly face.

"Two days," he said, "two whole, clear days have passed, and there is no reply. What *did* he tell thee, Nell?"

"Exactly what I told you, dear grandfather, indeed."

"True," said the old man, faintly. "Yes. But tell me again, Nell. My head fails me. What was it that he told thee? Nothing more than that he would see me tomorrow or next day? That was in the note."

"Nothing more," said the child. "Shall I go to him again tomorrow, dear grandfather? Very early? I will be there and back before breakfast."

The old man shook his head, and sighing mournfully, drew her towards him.

"'Twould be of no use, my dear, no earthly use. But if he deserts me, Nell, at this moment – if he deserts me now, when I should, with his assistance, be recompensed for all the time and money I have lost, and all the agony of mind I have undergone, which makes me what you see, I am ruined, and – worse, far worse that that – have ruined thee, for whom I ventured all. If we are beggars –!"

"What if we are?" said the child boldly. "Let us be beggars, and be happy."

"Beggars – and happy!" said the old man. "Poor child!"

"Dear grandfather," cried the girl, with an energy which shone in her flushed face, trembling voice, and impassioned gesture, "I am not a child in that I think, but even if I am, oh hear me pray that we may beg, or work in open roads or fields, to earn a scanty living, rather than live as we do now."

The child's voice was lost in sobs as she dropped upon the old man's neck; not did she weep alone.

These were not words for other ears, nor was it a scene for other eyes. And yet other ears and eyes were there and greedily taking in all that passed, and moreover they were the ears and eyes of no less a person than Mr Daniel Quilp, who, having entered unseen when the child first placed herself at the old man's side, refrained – actuated, no doubt, by motives of the purest delicacy – from interrupting the conversation, and stood looking on with his accustomed grin.

The old man at length chanced to see him, to his unbounded astonishment.

Nell looked at the old man, who nodded to her to retire, and kissed her cheek.

The dwarf said never a word, but watched his companion as he paced restlessly up and down the room, and presently returned to his seat. Here he remained, with his head bowed upon his breast for some time, and then suddenly raising it, said, "Once, and once for all, have you brought me any money?"

"No!" replied Quilp.

"Then," said the old man, clenching his hands desperately, and looking upward, "the child and I are lost!"

"Neighbour," said Quilp, glancing sternly at him, "let me be plain with you. You have no secret from me now."

The old man looked up, trembling.

"You are surprised," said Quilp. "Well, perhaps that's natural. You have no secret from me now, I say; no, not one. For now I know that all those sums of money, that all those loans, advances, and supplies that you have had from me, have found their way to – shall I say the word?"

"Aye!" replied the old man, "say it, if you will."

"To the gaming-table," rejoined Quilp, "your nightly haunt. This was the precious scheme to make your fortune, was it; this was the secret certain source of wealth in which I was to have sunk my money (if I had been the fool you took me for); this was your inexhaustible mine of gold, your El Dorado, eh?"

"Yes," cried the old man, turning upon him with gleaming eyes, "It was. It is. It will be till I die."

"That I should have been blinded," said Quilp, looking contemptuously at him, "by a mere shallow gambler!"

"I am no gambler," cried the old man fiercely. "I call Heaven to witness that I never played for gain of mine, or love of play; that at every piece I staked, I whispered to myself that orphan's name and called on Heaven to bless the venture, which it never did."

"I thought," sneered the dwarf, "that if a man played long enough he was sure to win at last, or at the worst not to come off a loser."

"And so he is," cried the old man, suddenly rousing himself from his state of despondency. "I have no resource but you, give me some help, let me try this one last hope. Help me for her sake I implore you – not for mine, for hers!"

"I'm sorry, I've got an appointment in the city," said Quilp, looking at his watch with perfect self-possession, "or I should have been very glad to have spent half an hour with you while you composed yourself – very glad."

"I was so deceived by your miserly way, the reputation you had among those who knew you of being rich, and your repeated assurances that you would make of my advances treble and quadruple the interest you paid me, that I'd have advanced you even now what you want, on your simple note of hand, though I had been led to suspect something wrong, if I hadn't unexpectedly become acquainted with your secret way of life," said Quilp.

"Who is it," retorted the old man desperately, "that notwithstanding all my caution, told you? Come. Let me know the name – the person."

The crafty dwarf, stopped short in his answer and said, "Now, who do you think?"

"It was Kit, it must have been the boy; he played the spy," said the old man.

"How came you to think of him?" said the dwarf in a

tone of great commiseration. "Yes, it was Kit. Poor Kit!"

So saying, he nodded in a friendly manner, and took his leave, still chuckling as he went.

Poor Kit

Daniel Quilp neither entered nor left the old man's house, unobserved. In the shadow of an archway nearly opposite, there lingered one who having taken up his position when the twilight first came on, scarcely changed his attitude for the hour together.

At length he gave the matter up as hopeless for that night, and suddenly breaking into a run as though to force himself away, scampered off at his utmost speed, nor once ventured to look behind him lest he should be tempted back again.

This mysterious individual dashed on through a great many alleys and making for a small house from the window of which a light was shining, lifted the latch of the door and passed in.

"Bless us!" cried a woman, turning sharply round, "who's that? Oh! It's you, Kit!"

"Yes, mother, it's me."

"Why, how tired you look, my dear!"

"Old master an't gone out tonight," said Kit. "Worse luck."

"You should say better luck, I think," returned his mother, "because Miss Nelly won't have been left alone."

"Ah!" said Kit, "I forgot that. I said worse luck, because I've been watching ever since eight o'clock, and seen nothing of her."

"I wonder what she'd say," cried his mother, stopping in her work and looking round, "if she knew that every night, when she – poor thing – is sitting alone at that window, you are watching in the open street for fear any harm should come to her, and that you never leave the place or come home to your bed though you're ever so tired, till such time as you think she's safe in hers."

"Never mind what she'd say," replied Kit, with something like a blush on his uncouth face; "she'll never know nothing, and consequently, she'll never say nothing."

"Some people would say that you'd fallen in love with her, I know they would."

To this, Kit replied by bashfully bidding his mother, "Get out."

"Speaking seriously though, Kit," said his mother, taking up the theme afresh, after a time, "it's a cruel thing to keep the dear child shut up there. I don't wonder that the old gentleman wants to keep it from you."

"He don't think it's cruel, bless you," said Kit, "and don't mean it to be so, or he wouldn't do it — I do consider, mother, that he wouldn't do it for all the gold and silver in the world. No, no, that he wouldn't. I know him better than that."

"Then what does he do it for, and why does he keep it so close from you?" said Mrs Nubbles.

"That I don't know," returned her son. "If he hadn't tried to keep it so close though, I should never have found it out, for it was his getting me away at night and sending me off so much earlier than he used to, that first made me curious to know what was going on. Hark! what's that?"

"It's only somebody outside."

"It's somebody crossing over here," said Kit, standing up to listen, "and coming very fast too. He can't have gone out after I left, and the house caught fire, mother!"

The footsteps drew nearer, the door was opened with a hasty hand, and the child herself, pale and breathless, and hastily wrapped in a few disordered garments, hurried into the room.

"Miss Nelly! What is the matter!" cried mother and son together.

"I must not stay a moment," she returned, "grandfather has been taken very ill, I found him in a fit upon the floor —"

"I'll run for a doctor," said Kit, seizing his brimless hat. "I'll be there directly, I'll —"

"No, no," cried Nell, "there is one there, you're not wanted, you – you – must never come near us any more!"

"What!" roared Kit.

"Never again," said the child. "Don't ask me why, for I don't know. Pray don't ask me why, pray don't be sorry, pray don't be vexed with me, I have nothing to do with it indeed! He complains and raves of you. I don't know what you have done, but I hope it's nothing very bad."

The unfortunate Kit looked at his young mistress harder and harder, and with eyes growing wider and wider, but was perfectly motionless and silent.

"I have brought his money for the week," said the child, looking to the woman and laying it on the table, "and – and – a little more, for Kit was always good and kind to me. It grieves me very much to part with him like this, but there is no help. It must be done. Good night!"

With the tears streaming down her face, and her slight figure trembling with the agitation of the scene she had left, the shock she had received, the errand she had just discharged, and a thousand painful and affectionate feelings, the child hastened to the door, and disappeared as rapidly as she had come.

The poor woman, who had no cause to doubt her son, but every reason for relying on his honesty and truth, was staggered by his not having advanced one word in his defence.

Kit, insensible to all the din and tumult, remained in a state of utter stupefaction.

Escape

Next morning the old man was in a raging fever accompanied with delirium, and sinking under the influence of this disorder he lay for many weeks in imminent peril of his life.

The child was more alone than she had ever been before.

The house was no longer theirs. Even the sick chamber seemed to be retained on the uncertain tenure of Mr Quilp's favour. The old man's illness had not lasted many days when Quilp took formal possession of the premises and all upon them, in virtue of certain legal powers to that effect, which few understood and none presumed to call in question. This important step secured, with the assistance of a man of law whom he brought with him for the purpose, the dwarf proceeded to establish himself and his assistant, Brass, in the house.

Brass was an attorney of no very good repute in the city of London. Dust and cobwebs were among the most prominent decorations of the office of Mr Sampson Brass.

His clerk, assistant, housekeeper, secretary, confidential plotter, adviser, intriguer, and bill of cost increaser was Miss Brass – a kind of amazon at common law.

Miss Sally Brass was a lady of thirty-five or thereabouts, of a gaunt and bony figure, and a resolute bearing, which if it repressed the softer emotions of love, and kept admirers at a distance, certainly inspired a feeling akin to awe in the breasts of those male strangers who had the happiness to approach her.

The Adventurers Depart

Thursday arrived, and there was no alteration in the old man. But a change came upon him that evening as he and the child sat silently together.

He shed tears – tears that it lightened her aching heart to see – and making as though he would fall upon his knees, besought her to forgive him.

"Forgive you – what?" said Nell, interposing to prevent his purpose. "Oh grandfather, what should *I* forgive?"

"All that is past, all that has come upon thee, Nell," returned the old man.

"Do not talk so," said the child. "Pray do not. Let us speak of something else."

"Yes, yes, we will," he rejoined. "And it shall be of what we talked of long ago – many months – months is it, or weeks, or days? Which is it, Nell?"

"I do not understand you," said the child.

"It has come back upon me today, it has all come back since we have been sitting here. I bless thee for it, Nell!"

"For what, dear grandfather?"

"For what you said when we were first made beggars, Nell. Let us speak softly. Hush! for if they knew our purpose downstairs, they would cry that I was mad and take thee from me. We will not stop here another day. We will go far away from here."

"Yes, let us go," said the child earnestly. "Let us be gone from this place, and never turn back or think of it again. Let us wander barefoot through the world, rather than linger here."

"We will," answered the old man, "we will travel afoot through fields and woods, and by the side of rivers, and trust ourselves to God in the places where He dwells."

"We will be happy," cried the child. "We never can be here."

"No, we never can again – never again – that's truly said," rejoined the old man. "Let us steal away tomorrow morning – early and softly, that we may not be seen or heard – and leave no trace or track for them to follow by."

The child's heart beat high with hope and confidence.

At length the day began to glimmer, and the stars to grow pale and dim.

The child then took him by the hand, and they trod lightly and cautiously down the stairs, trembling whenever a board creaked, and often stopping to listen.

It was the beginning of a day in June; the deep blue sky unsullied by a cloud, and teeming with brilliant light.

The old man and the child passed on through the glad silence, elate with hope and pleasure.

Good Fortune for Kit

Kit walked about, now with quick steps and now with slow; now lingering as some rider slackened his horse's pace and looked about him; and now darting at full speed up a bye-street as he caught a glimpse of some distant horseman going lazily up the shady side of the road, and promising to stop, at every door. But on they all went, one after another, and there was not a penny stirring.

He was quite tired out with pacing the streets, to say nothing of repeated disappointments, and was sitting down upon a step to rest, when there approached towards him a little clattering jingling four-wheeled chaise, drawn by a little obstinate-looking rough-coated pony, and driven by a little fat placid-faced old gentleman. Beside the little old gentleman sat a little old lady, plump and placid like himself, and the pony was coming along at his own pace and doing exactly as he pleased with the whole concern.

As they passed where he sat, Kit looked so wistfully at the little turn-out that the old gentleman looked at him, and, rising and putting his hand to his hat, intimated to the pony that he wished to stop.

"I beg your pardon, sir," said Kit. "I'm sorry you stopped, sir. I only meant did you want your horse minded."

"I'm going to get down in the next street," returned the old gentleman. "If you'd like to come on after us, you may have the job."

Kit thanked him, and joyfully obeyed.

The pony stopped no more until he came to a door whereon was a brass plate with the words "Witherden – Notary". Here the old gentleman got out and helped out the old lady, and then took from under the seat a nosegay resembling in shape and dimensions a full-sized warming-pan with the handle cut short off. This, the old lady carried into the house with a staid and stately air, and the old gentleman followed close upon her.

They went, as it was easy to tell from the sound of their voices, into the front parlour, which seemed to be a kind of office. The day being very warm and the street a quiet one, the windows were wide open, and it was easy to hear through the Venetian blinds all that passed inside.

At first there was a great shaking of hands and shuffling of feet, succeeded by the presentation of the nosegay, for a voice, supposed by the listener to be that of Mr Witherden the Notary, was heard to exclaim a great many times, "Oh, fragrant indeed!"

"I brought it in honour of the occasion, sir," said the old lady.

"Ah, an occasion indeed, Mrs Garland; an occasion which does honour to me, ma'am, honour to me," rejoined Mr Witherden the Notary. "I have had many a gentleman articled to me, ma'am, many a one, but there was never one among the number, ma'am, attached as I have been to many of them, of whom I augured such bright things as I do of your only son, Abel."

"Chuckster, bring in Mr Abel's articles. I am about to sign my name, you observe, at the foot of the articles which Mr Chuckster will witness. You see how easily these things are done!"

In about a quarter of an hour Mr Chuckster (with a pen behind his ear and his face inflamed with wine) appeared at the door, and informed Kit that the visitors were coming out.

Out they came forthwith; Mr Witherden, leading the old lady with extreme politeness, and the father and son following them, arm in arm.

The old gentleman, Mr Garland taking his seat and the reins, put his hand in his pocket to find a sixpence for Kit.

He had no sixpences, neither had the old lady, nor Mr Abel, nor the Notary, nor Mr Chuckster. The old gentleman thought a shilling too much, but there was no shop in the street to get change at, so he gave it to the boy.

"There," he said jokingly, "I'm coming here again next Monday at the same time, and mind you're here, my lad, to work it out."

"Thank you, sir," said Kit. "I'll be sure to be here."

At this Mr Witherden whispered behind the nosegay to the old gentleman that he believed the lad was as honest a lad as need be.

"Now," said Mr Garland, when they had made some further inquiries of him, "perhaps I may want to know something more about you, so tell me where you live and I'll put it down in my pocket-book."

Kit told him, and the old gentleman wrote down the address with his pencil.

The old gentleman took his place and they drove away, waving a farewell to the Notary and his clerk, and more than once turning to nod kindly to Kit as he watched them from the road.

Kit turned away, but when he came to the corner of the court in which he lived, lo and behold there was the pony again!

He lifted the latch of the door, and walking in, found them seated in the room in conversation with his mother, at which unexpected sight he pulled off his hat and made his best bow in some confusion.

"We are here before you, you see, Christopher," said Mr Garland, smiling.

"Yes, sir," said Kit; and as he said it he looked towards his mother for an explanation of the visit.

"The gentleman's been kind enough, my dear," said she, in reply to this mute interrogation, "to ask me whether you were in a good place, or in any place at all, and when I told him no, you were not in any, he was so good as to say that —"

"That we wanted a good lad in our house," said the old gentleman and the old lady both together.

Whereupon, Kit was formally hired at an annual income of six pounds, over and above his board and lodging, by Mr and Mrs Garland, of Abel Cottage, Finchley.

The Travellers

It was not until they were quite exhausted that the old man and the child ventured to stop and sit down to rest upon the borders of a litte wood.

"We are quite safe now, and have nothing to fear, grandfather," Nell said.

When they rose up from the ground, and took the shady track which led them through the wood, she bounded on. The old man cast no longer fearful looks behind, but felt at ease and cheerful, for the further they passed into the deep green shade, the more they felt that the tranquil mind of God was there, and shed its peace on them.

At length the path, becoming clearer and less intricate, brought them to the end of the wood, and into a public road. A broken finger-post announced that this led to a village three miles off; and thither they resolved to bend their steps.

The miles appeared so long that they sometimes thought they must have missed their road. But at last, to their great joy, it led downward in a steep descent, with overhanging banks over which the footpaths led; and the clustered houses of the village peeped out from the woody hollow below.

It was a very small place. The men and boys were playing cricket on the green; and as the other folk were looking on, they wandered up and down, uncertain where to seek a humble lodging. There was but one old man in the little garden before his cottage, and him they were timid of approaching, for he was the schoolmaster, and had 'School' written up over his window in black letters on a white board.

"Speak to him, dear," the old man whispered.

Nell dropped a curtsey, and told him they were poor travellers.

"If you could direct us anywhere, sir," said the child, "we should take it very kindly."

"You're a young traveller, my child," he said, laying his hand gently on her head. "Your grandchild, friend?"

"Aye, sir," cried the old man, "and the stay and comfort of my life."

"Come in," said the schoolmaster.

Without further preface he conducted them into his little schoolroom, which was parlour and kitchen likewise. Before they had done thanking him, he spread a coarse white cloth upon the table, with knives and platters; and bringing out some bread and cold meat and a jug of beer, besought them to eat and drink.

By the time they were ready to depart, school had begun. The schoolmaster walked with them to the gate.

It was with a trembling and reluctant hand, that the child held out to him money, faltering in her thanks as she thought how small the sum was, and blushing as she offered it. But he bade her put it away, and stooping to kiss her cheek, turned back into the house.

They had not gone half-a-dozen paces when he was at the door again; the old man retraced his steps to shake hands, and the child did the same.

"Good fortune and happiness go with you!" said the schoolmaster. "I am quite a solitary man now. If ever you pass this way again, you'll not forget the little village school."

"We shall never forget it, sir," rejoined Nell; "nor ever forget to be grateful to you for your kindness to us."

They bade him farewell very many times, and turned away, walking slowly and often looking back, until they could see him no more.

Clear of town, they took a footpath which struck through some pleasant fields. It had been gradually getting overcast, and now the sky was dark and lowering. Large drops of rain soon began to fall and, as the storm clouds came sailing onward, others supplied the void they left behind and spread over all the sky. Then was heard the low rumbling of distant thunder, and lightning quivered.

Drenched with the pelting rain, confused by the deafening thunder, and bewildered by the glare of the forked lightning, they would have passed a solitary house without being aware of its vicinity, had not a man, who was standing at the door, called lustily to them to enter.

"What were you going past for, eh?" he added, as he closed the door and led the way along a passage to a room behind.

"We didn't see the house, sir, till we heard you calling," Nell replied.

"No wonder," said the man, "with this lightning in one's eyes. You had better stand by the fire here, and dry yourselves a bit. You can call for what you like if you want anything. If you don't want anything, you are not obliged to give an order. This is a public-house, that's all."

The night being warm, there was a large screen drawn across the room, for a barrier against the heat of the fire.

"Nell, they're – they're playing cards," whispered the old man, suddenly interested. "Don't you hear them?

"Do you hear, Nell, do you hear them?" whispered the old man again, with increased earnestness, as the money chinked upon the table.

"I haven't seen such a storm as this," said a sharp cracked voice of most disagreeable quality, when a tremendous peal of thunder had died away, "since the night when old Luke Withers won thirteen times running, upon the red. We all said he had the Devil's luck and his own, and as it was the kind of night for the Devil to be out and busy."

"Do you hear what he says?" whispered the old man. "Do you hear that, Nell?"

The child saw with astonishment and alarm that his whole appearance had undergone a complete change. His face was flushed and eager, his eyes were strained, his teeth set, his breath came short and thick, and the hand he laid upon her arm trembled so violently that she shook beneath its grasp.

"Bear witness," he muttered, looking upward, "that I always said it; that I knew it, dreamed of it, felt it was the truth, and that it must be so! What money have we, Nell? Come, I saw you with money yesterday. What money have we? Give it to me."

"No, no, let me keep it, grandfather," said the frightened child. "Let us go away from here. Do not mind the rain. Pray let us go."

"Give it to me, I say," returned the old man fiercely. "Hush, hush, don't cry, Nell. If I spoke sharply, dear, I didn't mean it. It's for thy good. I have wronged thee, Nell, but I will right thee yet, I will indeed. Where is the money?"

"Do not take it," said the child. "Pray do not take it, dear. For both our sakes let me keep it, or let me throw it away – better let me throw it away, than you take it now. Let us go; do let us go."

"Give me the money," returned the old man, "I must have it. There – there – that's my dear Nell. I'll right thee one day, child, I'll right thee, never fear!"

She took from her pocket a little purse. He seized it with the same, rapid impatience which had characterised his speech, and hastily made his way to the other side of the screen. It was impossible to restrain him, and the trembling child followed close behind.

"Sit thee down, Nell," cried the old man, "sit thee down and look on. Be of good heart, it's all for thee – all – every penny. I don't tell them, no, no, or else they wouldn't play, dreading the chance that such a cause must give me. Look at them. See what they are and what thou art. Who doubts that we must win!"

As he spoke he drew a chair to the table; and the other three closing round it at the same time, the game commenced.

The child sat by, and watched its progress with a troubled mind. Regardless of the run of luck, and mindful only of the desperate passion which had its hold upon her grandfather, losses and gains were to her alike. Exulting in some brief triumph, or cast down by a defeat, there he sat so wild and restless, so feverishly and intensely anxious, so terribly eager, so ravenous for the paltry stakes, that she could have almost better borne to see him dead. And yet she was the innocent cause of all this torture, and he, gambling with such a savage thirst for gain as the most insatiable gambler never felt, had not one selfish thought!

At length the play came to an end, and Mr Isaac List rose the only winner.

"Do you know what the time is?" said Mr Groves, the

landlord, who was smoking with his friends. "Past twelve o'clock."

"It's very late," said Nell. "I wish we had gone before. What would it cost, sir, if we stopped here?"

"Two good beds, one and sixpence; supper and beer, one shilling; total, two shillings and sixpence," he replied.

She decided, after a great deal of hesitation, to remain. She took her grandfather aside, and telling him that she had still enough left to defray the cost of their lodging, proposed that they should stay there for the night.

"If I had had that money before – if I had only known of it a few minutes ago!" muttered the old man.

"We will decide to stop here if you please," said Nell, turning hastily to the landlord.

The old man took leave of the company, and they went upstairs together.

At last, sleep gradually stole upon her – a broken, fitful sleep, troubled by dreams of falling from high towers, and waking with a start and in great terror. A deeper slumber followed this – and then – what! That figure in the room!

A figure was there. Yes, she had drawn up the blind to admit the light when it should dawn, and there, between the foot of the bed and the dark casement, it crouched and slunk along, groping its way with noiseless hands, and stealing round the bed. She had no voice to cry for help, no power to move, but lay still, watching.

On it came – on, silently and stealthily, to the bed's head. The breath so near her pillow, that she shrunk back into it, lest those wandering hands should light upon her face. Back again it stole to the window – then turned its head towards her.

The dark form was a mere blot upon the lighter darkness of the room, but she saw the turning of the head, and felt and knew how the eyes looked and the ears listened. There it remained, motionless as she. At length, still

keeping the face towards her, it busied its hands in something, and she heard the chink of money.

Then, on it came again, silent and stealthy as before, and, replacing the garments it had taken from the bedside, dropped upon its hand and knees, and crawled away. How slowly it seemed to move, now that she could hear but not see it, creeping along the floor! It reached the door at last, and stood upon its feet. The steps creaked beneath its noiseless tread, and it was gone.

The first impulse of the child was to fly from the terror of being by herself in that room – to have somebody by – not to be alone – and then her power of speech would be restored. With no consciousness of having moved, she gained the door.

Once in her grandfather's room, she would be safe.

It crept along the passage until it came to the very door she longed so ardently to reach. The child, in the agony of being so near, had almost darted forward with the design of bursting into the room and closing it behind her, when the figure stopped again.

The idea flashed suddenly upon her – what if it entered there, and had a design upon the old man's life! She turned faint and sick. It did. It went in. There was a light inside. The figure was now within the chamber, and she, still dumb – quite dumb, and almost senseless – stood looking on.

The door was partly open. Not knowing what she meant to do, but meaning to preserve him or be killed herself, she staggered forward and looked in. What sight was that which met her view!

The bed had not been lain on, but was smooth and empty. And at a table sat the old man himself, the only living creature there, his white face pinched and sharpened by the greediness which made his eyes unnaturally bright, counting the money of which his hands had robbed her.

The first idea that flashed upon her mind was flight, instant flight; dragging him from that place, and rather dying of want upon the roadside than ever exposing him again to such terrible temptations.

Half undressed, and with her hair in wild disorder, she flew to the old man's bedside.

"What's this!" he cried, fixing his eyes upon her.

"I have had a dreadful dream," said the child, with an energy that nothing but such terrors could have inspired. "A dreadful, horrible dream. I have had it once before. It is a dream of grey-haired men like you, in darkened rooms by night, robbing the sleepers of their gold. Up, up!" The old man shook in every joint, and folded his hands like one who prays.

"Not to me," said the child, "not to me – to heaven, to save us from such deeds. This dream is too real. I cannot sleep, I cannot stay here, I cannot leave you alone under the roof where such dreams come. Up! We must fly."

"Tonight!" murmured the old man.

"Yes, tonight," replied the child. "Tomorrow night will be too late. The dream will have come again. Nothing but flight can save us. Up!"

The old man rose from his bed, his forehead bedewed with the cold sweat of fear and, bending before the child as if she had been an angel messenger sent to lead him where she would, made ready to follow her.

She took him by the hand as if she feared to lose him for an instant and then she led him forth. Up the steep hill they toiled with rapid steps, and not once looked behind.

The Visitor

Besides becoming in a short time a perfect marvel in all stable matters, Kit soon made himself a very tolerable gardener, a handy fellow within doors, and an indispensable attendant on Mr Abel, who every day gave him some new proof of his confidence and approbation.

One morning Kit drove Mr Abel to the Notary's office as he sometimes did, and having set him down at the house, was about to drive off to a livery stable hard by, when Mr Chuckster emerged from the office-door, and cried, "Woa-a-a-a-a-a! You're wanted inside here."

Kit scraped his shoes very carefully, and tapped at the office-door, which was quickly opened by the Notary himself.

"Oh! come in, Christopher," said Mr Witherden.

"Is that the lad?" asked an elderly gentleman, but of a stout, bluff figure, who was in the room.

"That's the lad," said Mr Witherden. "He fell in with my client, Mr Garland, sir, at this very door. I have reason to think he is a good lad, sir, and that you may believe what he says. Let me introduce Mr Abel Garland, sir – his young master; my articled pupil, sir, and most particular friend."

"Your servant, sir," said the stranger.

"Yours, sir, I'm sure," replied Mr Abel mildly. "You were wishing to speak to Christopher, sir?"

"Yes, I was. Have I your permission?"

"By all means."

"My business is no secret; or I should rather say it need be no secret *here*," said the stranger, observing that Mr Abel and the Notary were preparing to retire. "It relates to a dealer in curiosities with whom he lived, and in whom I am earnestly and warmly interested. I have been making inquiries in the neighbourhood in which his old master lived, and I learnt that he had been served by this lad. I found out his mother's house, and was directed by her to this place as the nearest in which I should be likely to find him. That's the cause of my presenting myself here this morning."

He turned to Kit and said: "If you think, my lad, that I am

pursuing these inquiries with any other view than that of serving and reclaiming those I am in search of, you do me a very great wrong, and deceive yourself. Don't be deceived, I beg of you, but rely upon my assurance. The fact is, gentlemen," he added, turning again to the Notary and his pupil, "that I am in a very painful and wholly unexpected position. I came to this city with a darling object at my heart, expecting to find no obstacle or difficulty in the way of its attainment. I find myself suddenly checked and stopped short in the execution of my design by a mystery which I cannot penetrate. Every effort I have made to penetrate it has only served to render it darker and more obscure; and I am afraid to stir openly in the matter, lest those whom I anxiously pursue should fly still further from me. I assure you that if you could give me any assitance, you would not be sorry to do so, if you knew how greatly I stand in need of it, and what a load it would relieve me from."

Kit was then put under examination and closely questioned by the unknown gentleman about his old master and the child, their lonely way of life, their retired habits, and strict seclusion. The nightly absence of the old man, the solitary existence of the child at those times, his illness and recovery, Quilp's possession of the house, and their sudden disappearance, were all the subject of much questioning and answer. Finally, Kit informed the gentleman that the premises were now to let, and that a board upon the door referred all inquirers to Mr Sampson Brass, Solicitor, from whom he might perhaps learn some further particulars.

"Not by inquiry," said the gentleman, shaking his head. "I live there."

"Live at Brass's the attorney's!" cried Mr Witherden in some surprise, having professional knowledge of the gentleman in question.

"Aye," was the reply. "I entered upon his lodgings t'other day, chiefly because I had seen this very board. It matters little to me where I live, and I had a desperate hope that some intelligence might be cast in my way there, which would not reach me elsewhere. Yes, I live at Brass's – more shame for me, I suppose?"

"That's a mere matter of opinion," said the Notary, shrugging his shoulders. "He is looked upon as rather a doubtful character."

"Doubtful?" echoed the other. "I am glad to hear there's any doubt about it. I supposed that had been thoroughly settled, long ago. I'll not detain you any longer now," he said, putting a crown into Kit's hand, and looking towards the Notary. "You shall hear from me again. Not a word of this, you know, except to your master and mistress."

"Mother, sir, would be glad to know –" said Kit, faltering.

"Glad to know what?"

"Anything – so that it was no harm – about Miss Nell."

"Would she? Well then, you may tell her if she can keep a secret. But mind, not a word of this to anybody else. Don't forget that. Be particular."

"I'll take care, sir," said Kit. "Thankee, sir, and good morning."

Quilp's Plans

In his secret heart, Daniel Quilp was both surprised and troubled by the flight which had been made. His uneasiness arose from a misgiving that the old man had some secret store of money which he had not suspected, and the idea of its escaping his clutches overwhelmed him with mortification and self-reproach.

Rumours had already got abroad that the little girl was the child of great people who had been stolen from her parents in infancy, and had only just been traced. Opinion

was divided whether she was the daughter of a prince, a duke, an earl, a viscount, or a baron, but all agreed upon the main fact, that the single gentleman who was asking questions all around was her father.

Mr Quilp soon made out that the single gentleman had been seen in communication with Kit, and had no difficulty in arriving at the conclusion that the intent and object of his correspondence with Kit was the recovery of his old client and the child.

"I am suspected and thrown aside, and Kit's the confidential agent, is he? I shall have to dispose of him, I fear. But for the lad and his mother, I could get this fiery gentleman comfortably into my net and chubby, rosy Nell. At the worst, it's a golden opportunity not to be lost. Let us find them first, and I'll find means of draining you of some of your superfluous cash, sir, while there are prison bars, and bolts, and locks, to keep your friend or kinsman safely. I hate virtuous people!" said the dwarf, throwing off a bumper of brandy, and smacking his lips, "ah! I hate 'em every one!"

This was not a mere empty boast, but a deliberate avowal of his real sentiments; for Mr Quilp, who loved nobody, had by little and little come to hate everybody nearly or remotely connected with his ruined client; the old man himself, because he had been able to deceive him and elude his vigilance – Kit most mortally, for the reasons already shown. Above and beyond that general feeling of opposition to them, which would have been inseparable from his ravenous desire to enrich himself by these altered circumstances, Daniel Quilp hated every one.

He travelled to the Wilderness, and ordered tea in the wooden summer-house that afternoon for three persons; an invitation to Miss Sally Brass and her brother to partake of that entertainment at that place having been the object of his journey.

It was not precisely the kind of weather in which people usually take tea in summer-houses, far less in summer-houses in an advanced state of decay, and overlooking the slimy banks of a great river at low water. Nevertheless, it was in this choice retreat that Mr Quilp ordered a cold collation to be prepared, and it was beneath its cracked and leaky roof that he in due course of time received Mr Sampson and his sister Sally.

"You're fond of the beauties of nature," said Quilp, with a grin. "Is this charming, Brass? Is it unusual, unsophisticated, primitive?"

"It's delightful indeed, sir," replied the lawyer.

"Cool?" said Quilp.

"N-not particularly so, I think, sir," rejoined Brass, with his teeth chattering in his head.

"Perhaps a little damp?" said Quilp.

"Just damp enough to be cheerful, sir," rejoined Brass. "Nothing more, sir, nothing more."

"And Sally?" said the delighted dwarf. "Does *she* like it?"

"She'll like it better," returned that strong-minded lady, "when she has tea; so let us have it."

"Sweet Sally!" cried Quilp, extending his arms as if about to embrace her. "A word," he said, "before we go further. Sally, hark'ee for a minute."

Miss Sally drew closer.

"Business," said the dwarf, glancing from brother to sister. "Very private business. Lay your heads together when you're by yourselves."

"Certainly, sir," returned Brass.

"There's a lad named Kit —"

Miss Sally nodded, implying that she knew of him.

"Kit!" said Mr Sampson. "Kit! Ha! I've heard the name before, but I don't exactly call to mind — I don't exactly —"

"You're as slow as a tortoise, and more thick-headed

than a rhinoceros," returned his obliging client with an impatient gesture.

"Don't let's have any wrangling," said Miss Sally, staying his hand. "I've showed you that I know him, and that's enough."

"She's always foremost!" said the dwarf, patting her on the back and looking contemptuously at Sampson. "I don't like Kit, Sally."

"Nor I," rejoined Miss Brass.

"Nor I," said Sampson.

"Why, that's right!" cried Quilp. "Half our work is done already. This Kit is one of your honest people, one of your fair characters; a prowling prying hound; a hypocrite; a double-faced, white-livered, sneaking spy; a crouching cur to those that feed and coax him, and a barking yelping dog to all besides."

"Fearfully eloquent!" cried Brass, with a sneeze. "Quite appalling!"

"Come to the point," said Miss Sally, "and don't talk so much."

"Right again!" exclaimed Quilp, with another contemptuous look at Sampson. "Always foremost! I say, Sally, he is a yelping, insolent dog to all besides, and most of all, to me. In short, I owe him a grudge."

"That's enough, sir," said Sampson.

"No, it's not enough, sir," sneered Quilp; "will you hear me out? Besides that I owe him a grudge on that account, he thwarts me at this minute, and stands between me and an end which might otherwise prove a golden one to us all. Apart from that, I repeat that he crosses my humour, and I hate him. Now, you know the lad, and can guess the rest. Devise your own means of putting him out of my way, and execute them. Shall it be done?"

"It shall, sir," said Sampson.

"Then give me your hand," retorted Quilp. "Sally, girl,

yours. I rely as much or more, on you than him."

The Trick

"Mr Richard, sir, good morning. Here we are again, sir, entering upon another day, with our bodies strengthened by slumber and breakfast, and our spirits fresh and flowing."

While he addressed his clerk in these words, Mr Brass was somewhat ostentatiously engaged in minutely examining and holding up against the light a five-pound bank note, which he had brought in, in his hand.

He laid the bank-note upon the desk among some papers, in an absent manner, and thrust his hands into his pockets. Richard Swiveller pointed to it, and warned him to take it up.

"No, Mr Richard, sir," rejoined Brass with emotion. "I will not take it up. I will let it lie there, sir. To take it up, Mr Richard, sir, would imply a doubt of you; and in you, sir, I have unlimited confidence. We will let it lie there, sir, if you please, and we will not take it up by any means." With that, Mr Brass patted him twice or thrice upon the shoulder, in a most friendly manner, and entreated him to believe that he had as much faith in his honesty as he had in his own.

Just then some person knocked at the office-door; and Kit looked in. "Is the gentleman upstairs, sir, if you please?"

"Yes, Kit," said Brass. "I am glad to see you, Kit, I am rejoiced to see you. Look in again, as you come downstairs, Kit."

When Kit, having discharged his errand, came downstairs from the single gentleman's apartment after the lapse of a quarter of an hour or so, Mr Sampson Brass was alone in the office. He was not singing as usual, nor was he seated at his desk. The open door showed him standing before the fire with his back towards it, and looking so very strange that Kit supposed he must have been suddenly taken ill.

"Is anything the matter, sir?" said Kit.

"Matter!" cried Brass. "No!"

"You are so very pale," said Kit, "that I should hardly have known you."

"Pooh, pooh! mere fancy," cried Brass.

"I have been thinking, Kit," said the lawyer, "that I could throw some employment your mother's way – you have a mother, I think? If I recollect right, you told me –"

"Oh yes, sir, yes, certainly."

"A widow, I think? An industrious widow?"

"A harder-working woman or a better mother never lived, sir."

"Ah!" cried Brass. "That's affecting, truly affecting. Put down your hat, Kit."

"Thank you, sir, I must be going directly."

"Put it down while you stay, at any rate," said Brass, taking it from him and making some confusion among the papers in finding a place for it on the desk. "I was thinking, Kit, that we have often houses to let for people we are concerned for, and matters of that sort. Now you know we're obliged to put people into those houses to take care of 'em – very often undeserving people that we can't depend upon. What's to prevent our having a person that we can depend upon, and enjoying the delight of doing a good action at the same time? I say, what's to prevent our employing this worthy woman, your mother? What with one job and another, there's lodging – and good lodging too – pretty well all the year round, rent free, and a weekly allowance beside, Kit. Now what do you think of that? Do you see any objection? My only desire is to serve you, Kit; therefore if you do, say so freely."

As Brass spoke, he moved the hat twice or thrice, and shuffled among the papers again, as if in search of

something.

"How can I see any objection to such a kind offer, sir?" replied Kit with his whole heart. "I don't know how to thank you, sir, I don't indeed."

"Why then," said Brass, suddenly turning upon him and thrusting his face close to Kit's with such a repulsive smile that the latter, even in the very height of his gratitude, drew back startled. "Why then, *it's done.*"

Kit looked at him in some confusion.

"Done, I say," added Sampson, rubbing his hands and veiling himself again in his usual oily manner. "Ha, ha! and so you shall find, Kit, so you shall find. But dear me, what a time Mr Richard is gone! A sad loiterer to be sure! Will you mind the office one minute while I run upstairs? Only one minute. I'll not detain you an instant longer, on any account, Kit."

Talking as he went, Mr Brass bustled out of the office, and in a very short time returned. Mr Swiveller came back almost at the same instant; and Kit left the room hastily to make up for lost time.

"He has minded the office," said Brass. "He has had my confidence, and he shall continue to have it; he — why, where's the —"

"What have you lost?" inquired Mr Swiveller.

"Dear me!" said Brass, slapping all his pockets one after another, and looking into his desk, and under it, and upon it, and wildly tossing the papers about. "The note, Mr Richard, sir, the five-pound note – what can have become of it? I laid it down here – God bless me!"

Mr Swiveller and Sampson Brass caught up their hats and rushed out into the street – daring along in the middle of the road, and dashing aside all obstructions as though they were running for their lives.

It happened that Kit had been running too, though not so fast, and having the start of them by some few minutes, was a good distance ahead. As they were pretty certain of the road he must have taken, however, and kept on at a great pace, they came up with him, at the very moment when he had taken breath, and was breaking into a run again.

"Stop!" cried Sampson, laying his hand on one shoulder, while Mr Swiveller pounced upon the other. "Not so fast, sir. You're in a hurry?"

"Yes, I am," said Kit, looking from one to the other in great surprise.

"I – I – can hardly believe it," panted Sampson, "but something of value is missing from the office. I hope you don't know what."

"Know what! good Heaven, Mr Brass!" cried Kit, trembling from head to foot; "you don't suppose –"

"No, no," rejoined Brass quickly, "I don't suppose anything. Don't say I said you did."

"Search me," said Kit, proudly, holding up his arms. "But mind, sir – I know you'll be sorry for this, to the last day of your life."

"It is certainly a very painful occurrence," said Brass with a sigh, as he dived into one of Kit's pockets, and fished up a miscellaneous collection of small articles; "very painful. Nothing here, Mr Richard, sir, all perfectly satisfactory. Nor here, sir. Nor in the waistcoat, Mr Richard, nor in the coat tails. So far, I am rejoiced, I am sure."

Richard Swiveller, holding Kit's hat in his hand, was watching the proceedings with great interest, and bore upon his face the slightest possible indication of a smile, as Brass, shutting one of his eyes, looked with the other up the inside of one of the poor fellow's sleeves as if it were a telescope, and bade him search the hat.

An exclamation, at once from Richard Swiveller and Kit himself, cut the lawyer short. He turned his head, and saw Dick standing with the bank-note in his hand.

"In the hat?" cried Brass, in a sort of shriek.

"Under the handkerchief, and tucked beneath the lining," said Dick, aghast at the discovery.

Mr Brass looked at Kit, who stood quite stupefied and motionless.

"And this," cried Sampson, clasping his hands, "this is the villain that I was going to benefit with all my little arts. A constable, sir, if you please!"

On arrival, the constable, holding Kit and pushing him on a little before him, so as to keep him at about three-quarters of an arm's length in advance, thrust him into a vehicle and followed himself. Sampson Brass got upon the box, and made the coachman drive on.

Still completely stunned by the sudden and terrible change which had taken place in his affairs, Kit sat gazing out of the coach window, almost hoping to see some monstrous phenomenon in the streets which might give him reason to believe he was in a dream.

Dream-like as the story was, it was true. He stood charged with robbery; the note had been found upon him, though he was innocent in thought and deed; and they were carrying him back, a prisoner.

All at once, as though it had been conjured up by magic, he became aware of the face of Quilp.

And what a leer there was upon the face! It was from the open window of a tavern that it looked out; and the dwarf had so spread himself over it, with his elbows on the window-sill and his head resting on both his hands, that what between this attitude and his being swollen with suppressed laughter, he looked puffed and bloated into twice his usual breadth. Mr Brass on recognising him immediately stopped the coach. As it came to a halt directly opposite to where he stood, the dwarf pulled off his hat, and saluted the party with a hideous and grotesque politeness.

"Aha!" he cried. "Where now, Brass? Where now? Dick? Pleasant Dick! And Kit? Honest Kit!"

"He's extremely cheerful!" said Brass to the coachman. "Very much so! Ah, sir – a sad business! Never believe in honesty any more, sir."

"Why not?" returned the dwarf. "Why not, you rogue of a lawyer, why not?"

"Bank-note lost in our office, sir," said Brass, shaking his head. "Found in his hat, sir – he previously left alone there – no mistake at all, sir – chain of evidence complete – not a link wanting."

"What!" cried the dwarf, leaning half his body out of window. "Kit a thief! Kit a thief! Ha, ha, ha! Why, he's an uglier-looking thief than can be seen anywhere for a penny. Eh, Kit – eh? Ha, ha, ha! Have you taken Kit into custody before he had time and opportunity to beat me! Eh, Kit, eh?"

With such good wishes and farewells, poured out in a rapid torrent until they were out of hearing, Quilp suffered them to depart; and when he could see the coach no longer, drew in his head, and rolled upon the ground in an ecstasy of enjoyment.

An Old Friend

Day followed day and always morning came.

The child had not only to endure the accumulated hardships of their destitute condition, but to bear the reproaches of her grandfather, who began to murmur at having been led away from their late abode and demand that they be returned to it. Now penniless, Nell felt a hopelessness of their ever being extricated together from their miserable wanderings, a dull conviction that she was very ill, perhaps dying; but no fear or anxiety.

A loathing of food, that she was not conscious of until

they expended their last penny in the purchase of another loaf, prevented her partaking even of this poor meal. Her grandfather ate greedily, which she was glad to see.

Their way lay through the same scenes as yesterday, with no variety or improvement. There was the same thick air, difficult to breathe; the same blighted ground, the same hopeless prospect, the same misery and distress. Objects appeared more dim, the noise less, the path more rugged and uneven, for sometimes she stumbled, and became roused, as it were, in the effort to prevent herself from falling. Poor child! the cause was in her tottering feet.

Towards the afternoon, her grandfather complained bitterly of hunger.

With less and less of hope or strength, as they went on, but with an undiminished resolution not to betray by any word or sign her sinking state, so long as she had energy to move, the child throughout the remainder of that hard day compelled herself to proceed; not even stopping to rest as frequently as usual, to compensate in some measure for the tardy pace at which she was obliged to walk. Evening was drawing on, but had not closed in, when – still travelling among the same dismal objects – they came to a busy town.

Faint and spiritless as they were, its streets were insupportable. After humbly asking for relief at some few doors and being refused, they agreed to make their way out of it as speedily as they could, and see if the inmates of any lone house beyond would have more pity on their exhausted state.

They were dragging themselves along through the last street, and the child felt that the time was close at hand when her enfeebled powers would bear no more. There appeared before them, at this juncture, going in the same direction as themselves, a traveller on foot, who, with a case strapped to his back, leant upon a stout stick as he

walked, and read from a book which he held in his other hand.

It was not an easy matter to come up with him, and beseech his aid, for he walked fast, and was a little distance in advance. At length he stopped to look more attentively at some passage in his book. Animated with a ray of hope, the child shot on before her grandfather, and, going close to the stranger without rousing him by the sound of her footsteps, began in a few faint words to implore his help.

He turned his head, the child clapped her hands together, uttered a wild shriek, and fell senseless at his feet.

It was the schoolmaster. No other than the schoolmaster.

He threw down his stick and book, and dropping on one knee beside her, endeavoured by such simple means as occurred to him, to restore her to herself; while her grandfather, standing idly by, wrung his hands, and implored her with many endearing expressions to speak to him.

"She is quite exhausted," said the schoolmaster, glancing upward into his face. "You have taxed her powers too far, friend."

"She is perishing of want," rejoined the old man. "I never thought how weak and ill she was, till now."

Casting a look upon him, half-reproachful and half-compassionate, the schoolmaster took the child in his arms, and bidding the old man gather up her little basket and follow him directly, bore her away at his utmost speed.

There was a small inn within sight, to which it would seem he had been directing his steps when so unexpectedly overtaken. Towards this place he hurried with his unconscious burden, and rushing into the kitchen, and calling upon the company there assembled to make way for God's sake, deposited it on a chair before the fire.

A Watery Grave

Mr Quilp remained shut up in his hermitage, undisturbed by any suspicion, and extremely well satisfied with the result of his scheming. Being engaged in the adjustment of some accounts, he had not strayed from his den for two whole days. The third day of his devotion to this pursuit found him still hard at work, and little disposed to stir abroad.

The day, in the highest and brightest quarters of the town, was damp, dark, cold, and gloomy. In that low and marshy spot, the fog filled every nook and corner with a thick dense cloud. Every object was obscured at one or two yards' distance.

"So! That little job being disposed of," said the dwarf, coolly, "I'll read my letter. Humph!" he muttered, looking at the direction. "I ought to know this writing. Beautiful Sally!"

Opening it, he read, in a fair, round, legal hand, as follows: "Sammy has been practised upon, and has broken confidence. It has all come out. You had better not be in the way, for strangers are going to call upon you. They have been very quiet as yet, because they mean to surprise you. Don't lose time. I didn't. I am not to be found anywhere. If I was you, I wouldn't be, either. S. B."

To describe the changes that passed over Quilp's face as he read this letter half-a-dozen times would require some new language. For a long time he did not utter one word; but after a considerable interval, he contrived to gasp out, "If I had him here. If I only had him here – I should drown him! Too easy a death, too short, too quick – but the river runs close at hand. Oh! If I had him here! Just to take him to the brink, coaxingly and pleasantly – holding him by the button-hole – joking with him – and with a sudden push, to send him splashing down! Drowning men come to the surface three time, they say. Ah! To see him those three times, and mock him as his face came bobbing up – oh, what a rich treat that would be!

"And this, like every other trouble and anxiety I have had of late times, springs from that old imbecile and his darling child – two wretched feeble wanderers. I'll be their evil genius yet. And you, sweet Kit, honest Kit, virtuous, innocent Kit, look to yourself. Where I hate, I bite. I hate you, my darling fellow, with good cause, and proud as you are tonight, I'll have my turn. What's that!"

A knocking at the gate. A loud and violent knocking. Then a pause; as if those who knocked had stopped to listen. Then the noise again, more clamorous and importunate than before.

"So soon!" said the dwarf. "And so eager! I am afraid I shall disappoint you. It's well I'm quite prepared. Sally, I thank you!"

The noise at the gate still continuing, he felt his way to the door, and stepped into the open air.

It was about eight o'clock; but the dead of the darkest night would have been as noon-day, in comparison with the thick cloud which then rested upon the earth, and shrouded everything from view. He darted forward for a few paces, as if into the mouth of some dim yawning cavern; then, thinking he had gone wrong, changed the direction of his steps; then stood still, not knowing where to turn.

"If I could find a wall or fence," said the dwarf, stretching out his arms, and walking slowly on, "I should know which way to turn. A good, black, devil's night this, to have my dear friend here. If I had but that wish, it might, for anything I cared, never be day again."

As the word passed his lips, he staggered and fell; and

next moment was fighting with the cold, dark water.

It was of no avail. The strong tide filled his throat, and bore him on, upon its rapid current. Another mortal struggle, and he was up again, beating the water with his hands. One loud cry now – but the resistless water bore him down before he could give it utterance, and, driving him under it, carried away a corpse.

Good News for Kit

By degrees they let Kit know that doubts have arisen, that inquiries are to be made, and perhaps he may be pardoned after all. At last, the evening being come, they bring him to a room where some gentlemen are assembled. Foremost among them is his good old master, who comes and takes him by the hand. He hears that his innocence is established, and that he is pardoned. He cannot see the speaker, but he turns towards the voice, and in trying to answer, falls down insensible.

Mr Garland, taking him into a room where they could be alone, told him that he had something yet to say, which would surprise him greatly. Kit looked so anxious and turned so pale on hearing this, that the old gentleman hastened to add that he would be agreeably surprised; and asked him if he would be ready next morning for a journey.

"For a journey, sir!" cried Kit.

"In company with me and my friend in the next room. Can you guess its purpose?"

Kit turned paler yet, and shook his head.

"Oh yes. I think you do already," said his master. "Try."

Kit murmured something rather rambling and unintelligible, but he plainly pronounced the words, "Miss Nell," three or four times – shaking his head while he did so, as if he would add there was no hope of that.

"The place of their retreat is indeed discovered," he said.

"And that is our journey's end."

Kit faltered out such questions as where was it, and how had it been found, and how long since, and was she well, and happy?

"I trust she will be soon. She has been weak and ailing. In the meantime," said the old gentleman, rising and laying his hand on Kit's shoulder, "you have great need of rest, for such a day as this would wear out the strongest man. Good night, and may our journey have a prosperous ending!"

Kit was no sluggard next morning, but springing from his bed some time before day, began to prepare for his welcome expedition.

Nor was he alone excited and eager. Before he had been up a quarter of an hour the whole house were astir and busy.

Now the single gentleman and Mr Garland were in the carriage, and the postboy was in the saddle, and Kit, well wrapped and muffled up, was in the rumble behind.

It was a bitter day. A keen wind was blowing, and rushed against them fiercely; bleaching the hard ground, shaking the white frost from the trees and hedges, and whirling it away like dust. But little cared Kit for weather.

The two gentlemen inside, who were little disposed to sleep, beguiled the time with conversation.

The single gentleman turned to his companion and said, "Are you a good listener?"

"Like most other men, I suppose," returned Mr Garland, smiling. "Why do you ask?"

"I have a short narrative on my lips," rejoined his friend, "and will try you with it. It is very brief."

Pausing for no reply, he proceeded thus: "There were once two brothers, who loved each other dearly. There was a disparity in their ages – some twelve years. Wide as the interval between them was, however, they became rivals too soon. The deepest and strongest affection of both their hearts settled upon one woman.

"The youngest was the first to find this out. I will not tell you what misery he underwent, what agony of soul he knew, how great his mental struggle was, but when the time of trial came, he left his brother to be happy. The truth never passed his lips, and he quitted the country.

"The elder brother married her. She was in Heaven before long, and left him with an infant daughter.

"In this daughter, the mother lived again. She grew to

womanhood, and gave her heart to one who could not know its worth.

"Through all the misery which followed this union; through all the cold neglect and through all the poverty he brought upon her, she never bewailed her fate. Patient to the last, she died a widow of some three weeks' date, leaving to her father's care two orphans; one a son of ten or twelve years old; the other a girl – an infant child.

"The elder brother, grandfather to these two children, was now a broken man; crushed and borne down by the heavy hand of sorrow. With the wreck of his possessions, he began to trade – in pictures first, and then in curious ancient things.

"The boy soon spurned the shelter of his roof, and sought associates more congenial to his taste. The old man and the girl dwelt alone together.

"The younger brother had made his pilgrimage through life alone. His voluntary banishment had been misconstrued, and communication between him and the elder often failed.

"Then, dreams of their young, happy life visited his pillow yet oftener than before. He settled his affairs and, with honourable wealth enough for both, arrived one evening at his brother's door!"

The narrator, whose voice had faltered lately, stopped. "The rest," said Mr Garland, pressing his hand, "I know."

Sad Reunion

"This is the place, gentlemen," said the driver, dismounting from his horse, and knocking at the door of a little inn. "Hallo! Past twelve o'clock is the dead of night here."

The dull, red glow of a wood fire showed them a figure, seated on the hearth with its back towards them, bending over the fitful light.

The form was that of an old man, his white head akin in colour to the mouldering embers upon which he gazed. And the failing light and dying fire, the time-worn room, the solitude, and wasted life, and gloom, were all in fellowship. Ashes, and dust, and ruin!

Kit tried to speak, and did pronounce some words, though what they were he scarcely knew. Still the same terrible low cry went on – still the same rocking in the chair – the same stricken figure was there, unchanged and heedless of his presence.

He had his hand upon the latch, when something in the form – distinctly seen as one log broke and fell, and, as it fell, blazed up – arrested it. He returned to where he had stood before – advanced a pace – another – another still. Another, and he saw the face. Yes! Changed as it was, he knew it well.

"Master!" he cried, stooping on one knee and catching at his hand. "Dear master. Speak to me!"

The old man turned slowly towards him; and muttered, in a hollow voice, "This is another! How many of these spirits there have been tonight!"

"No spirit, master. No one but your old servant. You know me now, I am sure? Miss Nell – where is she – where is she?"

"They all say that!" cried the old man. "They all ask the same question. A spirit!"

"Where is she?" demanded Kit. "Oh tell me but that – but that, dear master."

"She is asleep – yonder – in there."

They watched him as he rose and stole on tiptoe to the other chamber where the lamp had been replaced. They listened as he spoke again within its silent walls.

He came back, whispering that she was still asleep, but that he thought she had moved. It was her hand, he said – a little – a very, very little – but he was pretty sure she had moved it – perhaps in seeking his. He had known her do that before now, though in the deepest sleep the while. And when he had said this, he dropped into his chair again, and clasping his hands above his head, uttered a cry never to be forgotten.

For she was dead. There, upon her little bed, she lay at rest. The solemn stillness was no marvel now.

She was dead. No sleep so beautiful and calm, so free from trace of pain, so fair to look upon. She seemed a creature fresh from the hand of God, and waiting for the breath of life; not one who had lived and suffered death.

Her couch was dressed with here and there some winter berries and green leaves, gathered in a spot she had been used to favour. "When I die, put near me something that has loved the light, and had the sky above it always." Those were her words.

She was dead. Dear, gentle, patient, noble Nell, was dead.

Where were the traces of her early cares, her sufferings, and fatigues? All gone. Sorrow was dead indeed in her, but peace and perfect happiness were born; imaged in her tranquil beauty and profound repose.

When morning came, they heard how her life had closed.

She had been dead two days. She died soon after daybreak.

She would like to see poor Kit, she had often said of late. She wished there was somebody to take her love to Kit.

For the rest, she had never murmured or complained; but, with a quiet mind, and manner quite unaltered – faded like the light upon a summer's evening.

Along the path they bore her, and the old church received her in its quiet shade.

They carried her to one old nook, and laid their burden softly on the pavement. The light streamed on it through the coloured window – a window, where the boughs of trees were ever rustling in the summer, and where the birds sang sweetly all day long. With every breath of air that stirred among those branches in the sunshine, some trembling, changing light would fall upon her grave.

Earth to earth, ashes to ashes, dust to dust. Many a young hand dropped in its little wreath, many a stifled sob was heard. Some – and they were not a few – knelt down. All were sincere and truthful in their sorrow.

For many days, the old man pined and moped away the time, and had no comfort. Whatever power of thought or memory he retained, was all bound up in her. He never understood, or seemed to care to understand, about his brother.

Dead! He could not hear or bear the word. The slightest hint of it would throw him into a paroxysm, like that he had had when it was first spoken. In what hope he lived, no man could tell; but that he had some hope of finding her again – some faint and shadowy hope, deferred from day to day, and making him from day to day more sick and sore at heart – was plain to all.

And thenceforth, every day, and all day long, he waited at her grave for her. When it grew quite dark, he rose and returned home, and went to bed, murmuring to himself, "She will come tomorrow!"

He would sit at night, pondering with a secret satisfaction, upon the flight that he and she would take before night came again; and would whisper in his prayers, "Oh! Let her come tomorrow!"

The last time was on a genial day in spring. He did not return at the usual hour. He was found lying dead upon the stone.

They laid him by the side of her whom he had loved so well; and, in the church, the child and the old man slept together.